WHIZZ POP, GRANNY STOP!

For Mark, with my love . . . x
T.C.
To the memory of Lilian King
and Mary Berger – the whizz-poppingest grannies
a boy could have hoped for.
J.B.

First published in 2012 by Nosy Crow Ltd
The Crow's Nest, 10a Lant Street
London SE1 1QR
www.nosycrow.com

ISBN 978 0 85763 131 2 (PB)

Nosy Crow and associated logos are trademarks and /or registered trademarks
of Nosy Crow Ltd.

Text copyright © Tracey Corderoy 2012
Illustrations copyright © Joe Berger 2012

A CIP catalogue record for this book is available
from the British Library.

Printed in Spain

3 5 7 9 8 6 4

WHIZZ POP, GRANNY STOP!

Tracey Corderoy

illustrated by

Joe Berger

nosy crow

My granny is quite different . . .

. . . of that there is no doubt.
In a world jam-packed with grannies,
you'd always pick her out.
Although I love her awfully much
sometimes I wish she'd be
a little less peculiar
and a little more like . . . me!

My granny likes to help me
when things don't go quite right.
She's got this special Helping Kit
she whisks out day and night.

"Oooh!" cries Granny. "Stubborn hair!"
And suddenly . . . whizz! Pop!

"Eeek!" I gulp. "It's gone all PINK!
Oh do please, Granny, STOP!"

My granny likes to help me when I have lots to do.
Like cleaning up my bunny's very whiffy piles of poo.

"There we go!" beams Granny,
as she whizzes it away . . .

"But Granny, where has Flopsy gone?
I wanted **him** to stay!"

My granny likes to help me when I am in a spin.
She whizzes out her Helping Kit and gives a little grin.

"Ah yes," she nods. "A dance for swans!"
And then I hear . . .

"Oh NO!" I flap,
as feathers sprout.
"Granny! Please, just STOP!"

So then my birthday came around.
"Let's make a cake!" I said.
"But let's not use your Helping Kit–
let's whisk and bake instead!"

We weighed and poured and sieved and stirred
and it was SO much fun!
"Yippee!" I cheered when it was cooked.
"Oh, look how WELL we've done!"

I took out Granny's sewing box
and found some bits of red.
"They're perfect for a party dress!"
my granny smiled and said.

We cut and stitched. Then, "LOOK," I cried,

"it fits just like a glove!"

"And though it's not quite dressy-shaped

it's made with tons of love!"

Party-time began at four.
The food looked such a treat!
"We made it all ourselves!" I cried.
"As much as you can eat!"

Then Granny painted faces, without her Helping Kit.
And when she went a little wrong, no one cared a bit!
We flapped like bats. We croaked like frogs –
the party turned quite wild.

"Just like parties ought to be!"
my lovely granny smiled.

My friends sang Happy Birthday

and trooped off home to bed.

But then I noticed all the mess.
"Oh Granny – look!" I said.
"Don't worry, dear," my granny grinned.
And suddenly . . .

And off we zoomed together
on a supersonic mop!

And when the day was almost done
I sat on Granny's knee.
She said she had just one more
little birthday gift for me.

My granny might be different,

but I would like to say . . .

... I really wouldn't have my granny
any other way!

HAPPY